# Yu the World

## Mission Istanbul

Yusuf Kerem Sahin

Kitab Press
2018

ISBN: 1948633000 (Paperback Edition)
ISBN-13: 978-1948633000 (Paperback Edition)

Library of Congress Control Number: 2018934524

Edited by Mustafa Sahin

Printed and bound in USA

First Printing February 2018

Published by Kitab Press

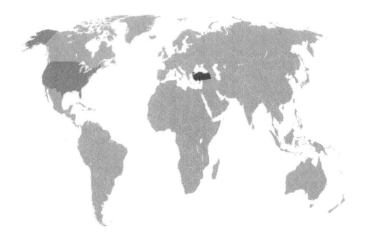

United States and Turkey. Credit: Wikipedia

# I.   PROLOGUE

Yusuf was born in Miami, Florida, the sunshine state. He now lives in Atlanta. His father is a professor and his mom is a teacher.

He has one young baby brother named Yahya, Turkish for John (the Baptist).

Did you know that Yusuf's parents are from Turkey?

The country, not the bird!

On his website, Yusuf explains how this bird got its name
and many other cool stuff.

Yusuf's dad was from a small historic town where Julius Caesar said "Veni Vidi Vici" (I came, I saw, I conquered).

Can you guess which town it is?

Yusuf's mom is from Istanbul, the biggest city in Turkey. Istanbul was the capital city of the Ottomans, the empire I mean, not the furniture!

Do you know where the name "Ottoman" comes from? Send your answers to Yusuf.

"How am I going to reach Yusuf?" you may ask. Check the next page!

Do you know where the name Ottoman comes from?

Come on! We are living in a social media world!

Follow him @YusufAroundTheWorld on Facebook or @YusufTravels on Twitter.

Check Yusuf's website YusufAroundTheWorld.com. for more information about the people and places discussed in this book.

By the way, currently Yusuf is finishing his second book on World War II.

If you want to a receive a free chapter from Yusuf's second book, and learn how he writes his books, send an email to info@YusufAroundTheWorld.com or subscribe to his free Readers Group at YusufAroundTheWorld.Com.

Anyways, it is exciting to read a book about the adventures of a kid from America who goes on an adventure to a country that is thousands of miles away.

...

It all started in Miami!

When Yusuf was a little boy, every week his parents would take him to Miami Beach, so that he would play in the sand.

It was a great family time. They enjoyed the breeze and the sound of the ocean. Yusuf loved the weather and the people in Miami.

Miami is home to a large Hispanic population, and Yusuf had many friends from South America. In the playground, he would greet his friends with a warm 'Hola.'

When Yusuf was four years old, they moved to Tampa, another Florida town northwest of Miami.

In Tampa Yusuf had a wonderful time. His daycare was in the New Tampa area. His days in the daycare were all blissful since he had a wonderful teacher called Ms. Joy. She was a caring person who taught Yusuf how to read and write his first letters.

After Tampa, they moved to Atlanta. So, by the time Yusuf started school in Atlanta, he has already developed an interest in learning new things and places. This made Yusuf a very curious kid who loved to read, think, and write.

When he was in first grade, Yusuf wrote his first book on Sharks. He wrote this seven-page book while his dad helped him find the photos and print them, just like this one!

Ms. Adam, his first-grade teacher, loved the book so much that she encouraged Yusuf to write more. Yusuf wrote short stories here and there to become a writer.

When Yusuf was in third grade, he decided to send a letter to the President. Yes, Yusuf wrote a three-page letter to President Obama. Guess what? He responded! It was amazing!!!

Yusuf read a lot of books to be a writer. He read every book in the Magic Tree House, Hardy Boys, and Harry Potter series.

This is the story behind Yusuf's adventures.

Would you like to join him in his next adventure?

## II.  MAGIC IN THE ATTIC

Strange things happened after Yusuf decided to be a writer. It was right after his family moved into a new house in Atlanta.

In the early days, Yusuf had not many friends in the neighborhood, so he spent most of his time at home reading books. It took time to get used to his new home.

The attic was a mysterious place. Yusuf loved to go there and read when his father was working. Though, he was never alone there. Therefore, it was a mystery for him when nobody was around.

One hot Atlanta summer day, Yusuf was minding his own business. It was a really hot day outside. He understood why people called the city "Hotlanta!"

Suddenly Yusuf heard a noise coming from the attic. He did not know what was happening. His dad was not at home and his mom was busy with Yahya, Yusuf's baby brother.

It was the last day of the school and as a big boy, Yusuf thought he had to overcome his fears. He never dared to go there alone. He loved learning new things and going on adventures. But this was different.

He remembered the video he watched on the Internet where a stranger lived in the house for years without the homeowners ever knowing about it.

His father told him to fill his mind with good stuff, not crazy videos that would haunt his imagination, especially late at night. He wished he listened to his daddy not to watch stuff like that.

But he decided not to return from this exciting but equally scary adventure. He wanted to prove himself he could go up there alone and protect the house from alien invaders.

He took his latest edition Nerf Rival Zeus, geared up with a flashlight and ammunition, and went upstairs.

The attic was a dark place. It only had natural light during the day.

It was an unfinished attic. Therefore, Yusuf's father filled it with books, files, tools and other stuff shelved rack one after another.

You would go up to the attic ten steps through a dimly lighted staircase. Only after coming to the middle of the stairs you could turn the light switch on.

As Yusuf approached to the light switch, he thought he heard a sound. With the "click" of the switch Yusuf's heart beat like crazy.

He thought if there was a person there, he or she could hear his heartbeat.

"Who is it?" said Yusuf.

Other than the echo of his own voice, it was dead silence. Was it an owl, or may be a bat? Or a stranger hiding up there before they moved in?

Yusuf aimed his Nerf Gun at the boxes with his fingers on the trigger in case something jumps out to attack him!

Last time he came here with his daddy, he mentioned to Yusuf about how difficult it was to close the window opening to the roof. Yusuf wanted to see whether it was open.

He wanted to be sure it was locked so he could feel better that no stranger entered there from outside.

As he came at the top of the stairs, he thought he saw a shadow move. He clenched his fists with his Nerf Gun ready for a fight. He recited all the prayers he had memorized.

"Growing up is the ability to confront your fears" his father used to say. He wanted to go against his fears and grow up. As he walked past one of the book shelves his shoulder smacked the other light switch and the lights went out. The only source of light was from the *open window!* He stumbled upon a box on the floor and his arm hit one of the shelves. Then he saw the shadow of an object coming falling down from his right side.

It was like a slow-motion movie scene.

"Oh my…"

At first, Yusuf thought it was an alien invader that was going to attack him! He stood still and fired a couple of powerful Nerf balls into the unknown object. The object coming down from above was obscured by the sunlight from the open window.

In shock, Yusuf screamed like never. He threw himself to the floor saying the best prayer he learned from his mom, "I seek refuge in the Lord of men."

Mom said it was a protective gear against danger. He did not know what it meant, but he kept repeating it.

It was only a matter of seconds before he threw himself back, just missing the object which hit the floor right in front of him, creating a cloud of dust. His Nerf gun fell out of his hands.

As he slowly opened his eyes, he was not sure what to expect. Is it an alien invading the house or a stranger living in the attic? Can his latest edition of Nerf protect him? With the rest of the prayer in his tongue he saw a big box of ancient books lying on the ground.

He was relieved. He grabbed his Nerf Gun and turned on his flashlight. But after he stood up and dusted off his pants, his eyes glimpsed an old green, leather-bound book.

Little did Yusuf know these books were from an ancient collection of travel books about mysteries of strange lands in old times. He did not know that after opening the book, his life would change forever.

What do you think? Should Yusuf open the book or go back to his room and forget about this scary event that happened in the attic?

# III. CLUE

"The clue is always in front of your eyes."

Yusuf had never seen an old book like this one. After reading all of his books on a tablet, it was interesting to hold a vintage book in his hands.

The green leather binding gave an ancient feeling to the book as if inviting him to read it.

There was even a huge compass on the front cover. He had never seen anything like this. They looked like some sort of journaling books. But he was not sure.

Yusuf leaned down and slowly held one of the books up. He thought that the book, contrary to its old look, was sturdy and heavy.

He picked the book up and a smell of the beautiful jasmine flower came to his nose, turning his fears into excitement.

As he cleaned the dust on the cover, the title of the book appeared: 'The Book of Travels'. He has never seen a book title like that before.

He slowly read the author's name *Ev-li-ya Che-le-bi*. Yusuf never heard of it. "Another old history book of father's," he said.

Inside the book was the page with the title of the book, the author's name. Next was a list of places carved out in a beautiful calligraphy.

Yusuf moved his fingers on it and felt the print. It was a list of cities some of which he learned in the school but others he did not.

After quickly skimming through the list of places he got to the next page where there was printed a small handwritten note: "If you want to go on a mysterious Travel, ask for it three times."

Yusuf did not understand what it meant. He read it again. "If you want to go on a mysterious Travel, ask for it three times."

"What mystery, what travel? What is the hidden secret here?" Yusuf asked himself.

He did not know what to do. But then he remembered the stories his father shared with him. In his small town, his father solved the mysteries right away because, his dad told him, "the clue is always right in front of your eyes."

Rather than trying to find the clue elsewhere Yusuf wanted to figure out what is in front of his eyes.

What might be the secret keyword he needs to say for the mysterious Travel? But, he wasn't sure whether he really wanted to go on mysterious travel.

Was he supposed to leave his family? He could never leave his family. They were his everything.

How could he live without his baby brother Yahya? Every morning Yusuf would wake up to go Yahya's room and give him a kiss and talk to him and share stories with him.

He took a deep breath and decided to give it a try and see what happens. Still, he hesitated.

As he waited more the more doubtful he became. He didn't want to waste time.

But he needed to find the secret keyword first. He read the handwritten note one more time.

"If you want to go on a mysterious Travel, ask for it three times."

The only thing that looked different on the note was the word 'Travel.' It was written in a different form. His heart was beating like crazy again.

Yusuf moved his fingers on the calligraphy and with a quick *Bismillah* repeated it three times.

Trraavveell... Trravell... and Travel.

Everything sloweeed dooowwnnnn.

Something was about to happen.

Yusuf hoped that it would be a good one.

He dimmed his eyes and made one last prayer.

# IV. THE NEW FRIEND

"Tell me who your friends are and I'll tell you who you are."

As soon as Yusuf repeated "Travel" the third time, a light came out of the book and lightened the entire attic with beams of white stars and smoke.

Yusuf could not believe what was happening in front of his eyes. It was magical, like in the movies.

Something emerged slowly behind the light and smoke.... What was it?... Come on...

A tall slim mustached man with a small turban and a green mantle appeared before Yusuf. As it all happened in just seconds Yusuf could not believe it. He fell back on the ground, amazed.

"I am here *effendim*, how can I serve my master?" said this man in an ancient traditional outfit.

"Who are you? How did you get here? What are you doing in my house?" said Yusuf. He thought his nightmares came true that a stranger lived in the attic.

He got his Nerf Gun and shot the man until he ran out of Nerf balls, but they all went through him.

"What are you?"

"What was that?" The ancient-looking man asked.

"A Nerf Gun." Yusuf answered.

"A gun?" The man looked confused "I come with peace" he said, as if he's coming from an old movie.

"I am here to serve and help people who call for me."

"But I did not ask for your help!" exclaimed Yusuf.

"I appear only for those who asks for Travel with a sincere heart. I guess that is what you did and here I am." The ancient man explained.

Seeing that Yusuf was confused the ancient man realized that he had some thrust building to do.

"You may not think you need my help, but we all need one another as a human family. Everyone gives something to the community and everyone takes out."

"So how are you going to help me?" said Yusuf with a lot of question marks in his mind.

"I can teach you how to travel around the world. There must be a reason you called me and I appeared here rather than somewhere else. If you find what I teach helpful, maybe then you can take what you learn and share with others. This is how we all learn and grow together, right?"

Yusuf was getting excited. He thought "this dude is a marketing pro." It was like in the movies you meet with a magical figure and do interesting stuff together.

It was a great idea to travel around the world. He wanted to see where this talk will go.

"I guess you have a point here," said Yusuf, trying to look cool. "Maybe I should consider this. But first, who are you? Where are you from?"

"I am Evliya Chelebi from Istanbul, the capital city of the Great Ottoman Empire!"

"Nice coincidence, my mom is from Istanbul," shouted back Yusuf.

"What a nice thing that is; maybe this can be the basis for our friendship," responded Evliya, "See, we have more in common than you'd imagine."

Evliya told Yusuf that he traveled around the world, met with many people and learned different cultures.

He also mentioned that he spoke many languages like Arabic, Persian, Greek and Latin.

He continued his story by telling how he first visited every corner of Istanbul, taking notes about the things even the locals did not know. One day he saw a vision, and it changed his entire life.

Evliya did not talk much about it and Yusuf did not want to bother him thinking it might be personal.

After the vision, Evliya researched about the places he wanted to visit and traveled around the world. He wrote his experiences in a book called *'Seyahatname.'*

Yusuf understood the 'seyahat' part. It meant 'travel' in Turkish but did not know what the other part meant.

"What is Se-ya-hat... na-me?" said Yusuf.

"It means travelogue," Evliya explained. "a diary or a journal that I kept about the places I visited during my travels. I was great at recording my experiences," Evliya said.

"God gave us pen to write things down, not to keep them in our minds" Evliya said thinking nobody else ever said anything like that before. It made him proud about himself.

Yusuf asked Evliya what his name meant.

He said "it means a good friend."

Yusuf wanted ask many questions but Evliya silenced him since he didn't have much time.

"I only have limited time every time I meet with you. Besides, I can only meet with you every other day. There are a lot of kids willing to travel. Busy, busy, busy!!!"

Evliya opened a notebook he brought with him, "hmm, my last notes are from Cairo. This means the last place I visited was in Egypt. Where are we right now?" Evliya asked.

"Atlanta" Yusuf replied.

"Antalya? Do you mean the coastal city in Turkey?"

"No Atlanta, Georgia."

"You mean the country of Georgia, by the Black Sea, it is a great place too. I love it."

"No!" said Yusuf again, "Georgia in the United States."

Evliya seemed confused. He did not know any of these places. He talked about other things, trying to change the subject.

"Anyways, if you want to travel with me, our travel has to start with Istanbul, since it is the biggest city in the world."

"I thought it was New York," Yusuf said.

Evliya did not know New York either. He opened his journal went through some pages and said,

"I am familiar with a city which later became popular and big, called mmm," turning more pages, "Yes, it is here. New Amsterdam, built as a Dutch colony. I learned it when I was visiting Amsterdam…. sometime around October 1663. It was in a faraway place in the New World."

"1663!" Yusuf was amazed that Evliya Chelebi knew the origins of New York before it became New York.

"Yes, you are right. It was originally New Amsterdam. The Dutch established New Amsterdam as a port city. Later it became New York in 1664, the most famous city in the world."

"Really? Well, things have changed a lot since the last time I was around. During my time, Istanbul was the biggest city with over a million population. It was the best city in the entire world," Evliya added.

It seemed like he did not want to give just some information here and there. He wanted to make a point out of it but as he had limited time, he returned to his point.

"It was challenging for me to go other places leaving the lovely Istanbul behind. People thought I was crazy. Why would I leave the best city on earth for other places?"

Evliya turned into an old man going through the stories of his life, forgetting his own time limit.

"But I was looking for more, I felt alone in the crowd. Inside me I realized that I wanted something different, the real happiness in this world."

He said best things that happened to him were traveling, learning new things, and sharing with people. These are the keys to a fulfilling life!

"Having a selfish life did not work for me. I did not know what I was supposed to do on this earth. I did not know how I can change things in life. I didn't even have a specific goal or direction. But I continued to search until one day in Istanbul's historic Suleymaniye library I found a small book by the world's greatest traveler…."

"Marco Polo" screamed Yusuf, before Evliya could finish his sentence.

"Well, I've heard of him but the world's greatest traveler was Ibn Battuta," said Evliya.

"Ibn Battuta began his journey in North Africa and traveled all over the world. His travel book was 'A Gift to those Who Contemplate the Wonders of Cities and the Marvels of Traveling.' I thought this book was a gift from God!" repeating slowly "wonders of cities and marvels of traveling."

Evliya continued, "I was working for the Ottoman government, but I did not like it. There were many rules on how to walk, talk, stand up and sit down. I had a great life, but I wanted to be free. I wanted to go places, see the wonders of cities and experience the marvels of traveling. But I did not know how to start!"

He gave a break to take a deep breath as if he has a very important thing to share.

"It is only after I saw the Prophet in a dream and asked for his prayer and his support. I realized that only after the dream I made a firm decision and new doors opened for me."

Evliya said "I could have become a vizier, sultan's best friend, or even a famous scholar because I memorized the entire Holy Book at an early age."

"The entire book!" exclaimed Yusuf with a surprise.

"Yes," said Evliya, "did you know I could read all of it in less than eight hours by heart?"

Yusuf felt bad for himself since he only memorized half of a chapter that summer and it took forever to finish.

"I wanted to use my time and energy to see places and help others," said Evliya, waking Yusuf from his daydreaming.

"That's exactly what I want!" exclaimed Yusuf.

"Well," responded Evliya, "I started small with what I had in my hand and you can do this too. There must be a reason I met with you. If you come to Istanbul, Yusuf Effendi, we will have more time to discuss and I will share everything I know with you."

Yusuf liked the way Evliya called him "Effendi," Master.

"Where will I find you?" Yusuf asked.

"Well, do you know Fatih Mosque?" Evliya asked.

"Of course!" said Yusuf, "my grandparents live just around the corner there."

"That's great," said Evliya. He took out the map of the area from his pocket and continued while showing the location on the map.

"As soon as you enter the courtyard from the north side, make a left. Then go to the end of the east side."

Yusuf said, "I know where you are talking about. I used to ride my scooter every summer evenings where the people feed the pigeons."

"I don't know what *'ouskooteraya'* is but feeding the pigeons is an age-old tradition, I love to feed the pigeons too. That's why I make my appointments right by the bench where people feed pigeons. If you exit from the east gate of the mosque, you can see me right there waiting for you."

"Got it," said Yusuf.

"One last thing, or maybe two," added Evliya.

"What?"

"First, no to guns! We are people of peace!"

"Ok," said Yusuf, slowly dropping his favorite Nerf Gun down.

"Second, do not forget! As my name reminds me every day, I want to remind you too. Be friendly to everybody, make firm decisions and ask things only from God. He is the one that can open doors for you. Only after this, I and other good people will be at your service."

"Evliya is very religious," Yusuf thought. But before he could say a word, Evliya disappeared.

All of a sudden, Yusuf heard his mom trying to wake him up.

"Wake up Yusuf! What are you doing here?"

When Yusuf opened his eyes, he realized that he fall asleep in the attic holding Evliya Chelebi's Book of Travels in his hand.

"Where is Evliya?" screamed Yusuf.

Yusuf's Mom responded with a smile. "What are you up to, little monster? What were you dreaming? How did you learn about Evliya Chelebi?".

Yusuf wanted to tell her everything, but she continued before he could say a word.

"Ok, it is too late already. You made me worried. I have been looking for you all over the place. It is time to go to bed."

Yusuf went downstairs. His mom reminded him to brush his teeth and offer the night prayers before going to bed.

He thought it would be best to keep this secret to himself. He felt he became a big boy now that he has something to keep to himself and not share with anybody else.

If it was a bad thing he would have shared with his parents but this time he found it safe to keep it to himself. A sense of growing up filled inside.

During the night prayer, many things came to his mind. Yusuf was not sure when or how his family would go to Istanbul so that he could meet with Evliya.

He remembered Evliya's words and promised himself to be a good person, have good intentions and ask things only from God.

Yusuf opened his hands up and said "Oh God, I want to travel around the world. Please open good doors for me!" He felt much better and confident.

He found his life's mission.

# V. TRAVEL

"That who travels, finds health." Turkish proverb.

When Yusuf woke up the next day, it was six in the morning. He rarely woke up this early in the summer but this was different. He had a mission inside himself, a definite goal that gave him a direction.

He wanted to travel the world to help people and share his experiences with others, just like Evliya.

He made his bed and offered his morning prayer. It was a great feeling waking up early. He even found some extra time to read books and play with his toys before his mom shouted "Yusuf, breakfast is ready!"

"Coming Mom!" Yusuf responded back.

He went downstairs and got his plate from the shelf and sat on the breakfast table right next to his father.

"Good Morning Baba,"

"Good Morning *aslanim*!"

His dad loved to call Yusuf 'my lion.'

"Yusuf, how do you want to spend your summer?"

"I have many ideas, baba, but first I want to go to Turkey to visit my grandparents," Yusuf replied.

"Well, then let's do it,"

"Yay!" Yusuf said. "When can we go?" Yusuf asked.

"Let's decide on that." his dad replied. "Hmmm," he said and took tickets out of his pocket. Yusuf's dad apparently bought the tickets already!

"We are flying on Monday!!!"

Yusuf took the tickets and waved them like they were the Golden Ticket from Willy Wonka and the Chocolate Factory.

"Are you excited to see grandma and grandpa!!" said mom.

"Yeah! I can't wait!" Yusuf said

Yusuf spent the entire day packing up and getting ready. Next day he woke up early again. They were ready to go to the airport for Turkey.

Yusuf loved flying, especially after his life changing experience, it was definitely going to be great.

He was no more interested in the food served on board or the cartoons and movies he loved to watch while his parents had some rest.

This time, before he arrived in Istanbul, he wanted to learn as much as possible about Evliya Chelebi. It was a direct flight so Yusuf just had ten hours to read about Evliya and then make a plan about his summer adventures.

While his parents were getting ready to have some rest on the plane, to their amazement, Yusuf took a book out and began reading.

His parents were really surprised. His father especially wanted ask some questions, but he was tired and Yusuf was not engaging that much of a conversation.

But Yusuf's daddy was not there to quit. He turned to his wife. "This young fella is up to something!"

"Come on," said his mom "Leave him alone. Look at him. You are worried just because he began to read about the life of Evliya, world's most famous traveler?"

Without meaning she said "He is our little Evliya Chelebi!" She was right Yusuf wanted to be another Evliya!

From the book, Yusuf learned that Evliya was a highly educated person. He had ties to the Ottoman royal family. Ottoman Empire was the strongest country in the world.

He had a great job. Evliya studied different languages and cultures. He taught himself Arabic, Persian, Greek and Latin. Later he traveled all over the world leaving his job behind.

His travelogue became the longest ever written travelogue in the world, longer than that of Marco Polo and Ibn Battuta.

More importantly, he had a unique writing style which amused people. Until today he is by far the most famous historical personage of the Ottoman Empire.

Thanks to Evliya, people learned about the little known facts about other countries and people. Yusuf was so surprised that he did not know anything about him until Evliya showed up in his attic.

He couldn't be more excited. It was a marvelous thing that happened just a couple of days ago.

One small adventure in the attic led him to a series of life changing events. Yusuf was glad that he acted brave.

# VI. ISTANBUL

"If the world were one country, Istanbul would be its capital." Napoleon Bonaparte

Yusuf and his family landed at Istanbul's airport on a fine summer day. Yusuf's aunt Sajida and uncle Khalil met them at the airport. It was great to see them.

After picking up the luggage, they hopped on Uncle Khalil's car and headed off to the grandparents' house.

Airport was not far from Fatih, the neighborhood where Grandpa and Grandma lived. But heavy traffic made it feel like it was in another town.

On the way, Yusuf was able to catch up with his uncle and aunt. Uncle Khalil just finished the law school.

Now as a proud law school graduate, he wanted to come to the United States to get some more education. He loved the US and the American people. After all, his nephew Yusuf was an American.

Aunt Sajida, on the other hand, began working at a university as an "intellectual property" expert. Although Yusuf did not understand what it meant, he knew that she loved her job.

As they got closer and closer to the downtown, the traffic became more crowded and streets became narrower.

Yusuf could not understand how people drove cars here. Drivers acted like there were no lanes on the road. It was impossible to imagine something like that in America. But it was very normal for the locals.

"If you want to get anywhere," Uncle Khalil said, "you have to find a shortcut. Otherwise you get late."

He cut a couple of cars here, sped up there and made it an exciting ride for Yusuf.

Yusuf couldn't remember how many mosques, historical buildings and ancient ruins he saw during this short and hot ride. It was like going through an open-air museum.

It was getting hotter and hotter. Turks did not use AC as much as the Americans. Yusuf rolled down the window a little. He felt the afternoon breeze of this wonderful city on his face.

Yusuf visited Istanbul many times before. But after he met Evliya, the city looked like an entirely different place.

Everything he did not recognize before gave him a sense of awe, joy and excitement. He realized that looking and seeing are two different things.

Once again, he promised himself to stay true to his promise that he made yesterday: he will travel around the world, visit new places, meet with different people, learn their cultures, and help them as much as possible.

While his parents were discussing regular topics, Yusuf was in a different world in his imagination, accompanied by his new friend, Evliya.

When they arrived in the block where his grandparents lived Yusuf jumped out of the car and ran to the five story apartment building. He rang the bell to be the first person to see his beloved grandparents.

He pushed the door and Grandfather Ahmet and Grandmother Farida were waiting for him there. "Grandpa! Grandma!" Yusuf screamed with happiness.

"Yusuuuuuf!" grandparents said after giving a long and warm hug.

"We have a surprise for you" said Grandpa. He took out two gold coins and gave them to Yusuf as a gift.

"Thank you so much!" said Yusuf with a joy.

Grandpa gave gold coins to Yusuf every time he visited them. It was like a family tradition. Yusuf hugged his uncle and aunt again. It was a real delight.

Yusuf realized that being a family meant more than everything because families brought real happiness to people's lives.

Another amazing thing about the grandparents was the huge and ornate apartment that they lived in!

The entire family lived in the same building. The first floor was for the guests visiting the family.

Yusuf's grandparents had the third floor. Uncle Mehmet, lived in the penthouse. Uncle Mehmet was the father of Yusuf's favorite cousin Ahmet, named after the Grandpa.

Grandpa had two brothers who lived in other floors. Uncle Asim and his family lived in the second floor. He was a professor of Engineering. Yusuf loved Uncle Asim. That's why he called him Uncle "Awesome".

Uncle Ibrahim and his family lived in the fourth floor. He was a tall and handsome businessman who would travel a lot and bring interesting stuff for the family from all around the world.

The apartment building was a blessing for Yusuf. He could visit the entire without leaving the building.

It was a big deal compared to the lifestyle he had in Atlanta where visiting a friend or a family member would require a serious planning. He was so happy that everybody he loved so much lived in the same building.

# VII. ELEPHANT'S STORY

"I learned that courage was not the absence of fear, but the triumph over it. The brave man is not he who does not feel afraid, but he who conquers that fear."
Nelson Mandela

First thing Yusuf wanted to do next day was to meet with his cousin Ahmet. For that he needed a good night's sleep. But he was so excited that he couldn't even close his eyes.

He took a warm shower, brushed his teeth but still his heart was beating like a small bird.

He realized that he needed some help. He did not know what to do. He knew that he could not share his new adventure with anybody else.

While he was thinking anxiously about the unanswered questions, his mom came to the room to pick up something.

Yusuf was not sure. But he had to say something. He said," Mommy can I talk to you for a second."

"Sure," said his mother. She stood by the door ready to leave right away.

"I need to talk something important here with you." His mom got the message and closed the door and sat right by his side.

"Tell me baby, how can I help?"

After a pause, Yusuf said, "what did you do when you felt... mmm.... like when you were young... you know... a lot of things going on in life, adventures."

It was not even a full sentence. But right after he finished, he began to feel better already. It was like a burst of energy that he was able to let it go. He was happy that he shared it.

Mommy smiled at him making Yusuf feel that she understood what he was going through. It was a nice feeling to be understood.

She began to talk about a similar experience she had when she was Yusuf's age. Yusuf's eyes began to shine upon learning he was not alone. It happened to someone else in the family, more importantly to his mom.

"So, what did you do?"

His Mom said something that didn't quite make sense. She said "you have to live the experience fully, don't try to escape from it and see what will it teach you."

Yusuf wanted to feel calm and comfortable right here and right now but mommy told him to live it patiently and stick to it!

When Yusuf looked confused his mother said, "Son, life is a test, and there are many things beyond our control. If you want to be in charge of everything, if you want to know and control everything, you will fail."

Yusuf thought when you are in charge, you are the boss. When you control things, you are the king. But mommy said the opposite.

Yusuf's Mom realized that she has to clarify what she meant. So, she told him an exciting elephant story.

"Life is like a person riding an elephant," said Yusuf's mom. Yusuf was more confused.

"When a person rides an elephant, he or she tries to control the elephant as much as possible. But if the elephant decides to go its own way, there is no way that the rider can stop it," his mother said.

"There are times in life, things don't go the way we want. There is always some uncertainty. What we need to do is to continue to ride the elephant and try to see where it takes us."

She was up to something.

"Your job is NOT to be in control of everything. Your job is, not to give up but continue your travel. When you persist and stay on track, you will have a better understanding about what is going on."

She took a deep breath and asked "Do you know Rumi?"

Yusuf had no idea.

"Mawlana Rumi," said his mother "is a Persian Sufi poet who lived in Turkey. He is a great scholar. You should read about him."

I have to learn first about Evliya, Yusuf told to himself but continued to listen.

"Rumi says that," Yusuf's mother continued "as you start to walk on the way, the way appears."

"As you start to walk on the way, the way appears," she repeated. "You cannot know what comes next before you walk on that way! When you arrive the destination, you will realize that there was a reason why the elephant took you there."

She continued "Instead of making it miserable for you try to change it, you will see that behind that shaky ride there is always a great surprise."

Yusuf felt slightly better now. When his mom finished her sentence, Auntie Sajida's voice could be heard from the corridor.

"Abla, Yahya is crying, I guess he is asking for his pacifier."

Yusuf's mother jumped high up remembering that she was late. She hugged Yusuf tucked him in the bed and gave him a kiss on the forehead.

"Don't forget the elephant and the ride!" she said with a warm smile.

Yusuf thanked her.

As Yusuf's eyes were closing slowly, his lips began to repeat his nightly prayer.

Next day after breakfast Yusuf wanted to visit Uncle Mehmet's house to see his cousin Ahmet. They lived in the penthouse. Visiting Ahmet meant pillow wars, and they had a big share of it.

At one-point Yusuf got hit in the face by a pillow.

"Are you okay?" his cousins asked.

"Yes! I'm perfect!"

Then, they continued the war until it was late night. Late at night the entire family all gathered together and prayed the night prayer before going to bed.

Yusuf was as excited as before. But he was thinking about Evliya and the adventures.

Next day was Wednesday. It was the day of the Bazaar, the weekly farmer's market, or the *Charshamba Pazari* as the locals called it.

"Yusuf, do you want to go to the Bazaar with me today?" said his Grandma.

"Yesss!" replied Yusuf. He thought he could find a way to escape and get the chance to meet with Evliya as they planned previously. Yusuf and his grandma went out together.

Yusuf took his scooter with him thinking that it would be much faster to go around the town with the scooter. He had to be quick to have enough time to meet Evliya.

In the bazaar Yusuf assured his Grandma that if he is lost, he can easily find his way back to home.

This was the beauty of Istanbul. It was a huge city of fifteen million people yet inside the big city the neighborhoods functioned like safe environments for the kids and the families.

Everybody knew each other, if you were lost you could ask help from the neighborhood shop owner by just calling him "Uncle" or "Auntie," tell them your parent's name and they would go the extra mile to help you out.

As Yusuf and the Grandma continued to roam around the bazaar, Yusuf has seen many things he has never seen back in the States.

He has seen cherry in the States but sour cherry (*vishne*) was very popular in Istanbul. They were all fresh, organic and very cheap too.

In Turkey they use the metric system. So, instead of the pound (lb.) they used kilogram.

One kilo meant two pounds. Two pounds of sour cherry was just thirty cents. Or two pounds of his favorite fruit mulberry was just forty cents in Istanbul. Delicious!

While his grandma was enjoying her time with Yusuf and picking the freshest grocery items and sometimes haggling the price with the vendors, Yusuf turned around the corner and disappeared in the crowd.

Yusuf had mixed feelings about what he was up to. He was very excited that he will soon be meeting with Evliya.

He was not sure whether he really saw Evliya or it was just a dream. When his mom woke him up from his vision, he had some doubts about it. Was it a dream?

He had high hopes because when he woke up he was holding the book and the map that Evliya gave him.

So, he took the map out from his pocket and continued to ride his scooter eastwards towards the Fatih Mosque, the big historical mosque.

Now was the time to see whether it was a dream or not. Yusuf knew that he did not have much time and he had to be quick.

The streets were so crowded that Yusuf hit a couple of shoppers and food vendors on the way.

The mosque was very close, but it took him five to six minutes just to reach the stoned walls of the Fatih Mosque courtyard.

Fatih Mosque

As soon as he entered from the arc gate, he made a quick left turn to go on the north side towards the pigeon feeding area.

Just as he was trying to speed up on his scooter a huge dog began to chase him barking.

"Oh my God!" Yusuf screamed.

Yusuf did not know what to do. The dog was getting closer and closer yet Yusuf's scooter had limited speed.

As the dog was getting closer Yusuf could feel its breath on his neck.

Just around the time when the dog was going to leave a permanent mark on Yusuf's buttocks, a magical thing stopped the dog to a complete halt.

Yusuf taught it must be an Angel who saved him. Or was it Evliya? He was out of breath. He could not even look back for a while.

When he looked back, hoping to see his new friend, it was the long chain of the dog that was holding the angry monster away from Yusuf. Yusuf could not stop laughing.

"Sometimes magic comes in ordinary ways" he told himself and continued to follow the route on the map.

As he made the right turn at the northeastern corner of the mosque, to his surprise there were no abandoned old sitting areas as Evliya mentioned in the map.

He looked for the trees that showed in the map but it was all marble grounds no trees as if a big hurricane came here to sweep all the trees and replaced them with stones.

He was a bit confused because Evliya's description definitely did not match with the courtyard.

By the time he arrived there he was already exhausted. He tried to find a place to sit. He found a bench and sat there. He was excited to be meeting with Evliya. He opened the book and slowly whispered "Travel" three times.

Unfortunately, it did not work. He tried one more time, this time louder. Nope. It was a really heartbreaking experience for Yusuf because his newfound friend Evliya was not there. He did not show up.

Yusuf tried to keep his chin up decided to check around. He stood up and pushed his scooter down to the southwest side of the mosque. There was a huge crowd visiting a tomb. Yusuf passed them slowly to see whether Evliya was there. Nada!

He made another right turn and cruised to the southwestern side slowly riding his scooter passing where the people were taking ablution. No, he was not there either.

Yusuf found a quiet space and sat down. He felt a big breeze coming from the sea side, he could see the Marmara Sea behind all those huge apartments. He took Evliya's book out and repeated "Travel" three times.

The breeze touching his face made him feel the cool weather in the summer hot Istanbul. Yusuf felt the breeze in his face and opened his eyes slowly.

He opened his eyes with a hope but soon his joy disappeared because Evliya was not there.

He thought maybe he mispronounced the words, so he gave a try one last time.

"Trravvell, Trravvlel, Trravvellllll!"

Nope. One more time. Unfortunately not. It was a big shock for Yusuf because it was making his suspicions correct that maybe it was a dream that had nothing to do with reality.

The map that he had also could not match the mosque's courtyard. He couldn't help but crying.

"This is just a stupid dream," Yusuf told to himself crying.

It devastated him. That was the end it. All of his dreams are gone now. Traveling around the world, helping people 'blaa blaa blaa' began to disappear before his eyes.

He was alone at the heart of Istanbul, crying like a baby. As he could not realize his dream, he began to talk bad about it.

It was just a stupid thing Yusuf said to himself. As Evliya's book fell from his hand, he was continuing "Stupid, Stupid, Stupid…. "

While Yusuf was crying his grandmother was running around trying to find him. She threw away all the grocery she purchased from the bazaar looking to find her beloved grandson in sweat and tears.

Finally, she saw Yusuf in the courtyard of the Mosque. As soon as Yusuf saw his grandmother running towards him, he decided to play little grandson role turning his serious cry into a babyish one.

His grandmother ran towards him, also crying. She hugged Yusuf with a big relief.

Yusuf explained how he got lost and how things were different from the last time. His grandma consoled him and they began walking back home.

While clearing his tears, Yusuf asked his grandma how she found him.

"It is not difficult to find an American kid, with a scooter running over people and knocking down the vegetable stalls," she said smiling.

On the way back, all the people in the bazaar were looking at Yusuf. They were telling the grandma what Yusuf just did to them.

Yusuf's cheeks turned red, he felt a bit guilty but could not say anything. Sometimes silence is the best form of apology in this country. It looks like his apology was accepted and everybody was just fine.

# VIII.   AFTER HARDSHIP COMES EASE

In the evening Yusuf was in a bad mood. He didn't talk much. Worse, he did not talk to his cousin Ahmet, who came all the way to see him.

After the dinner, seeing that Yusuf was not in the mood, his mom offered him to go to the neighborhood ice cream shop.

"What do you think if we go buy ice-cream?" she asked.

"Of course, it is delicious!" Aunt Sajida joined them.

The ice-cream shop was a local place *Baltepe* meaning "Honey Hill" in Turkish. It was on a busy corner in the town center right next to the neighborhood park.

They all walked to the ice cream shop under the evening breeze. Yusuf ordered his favorite vanilla chocolate while mom and auntie got their favorite plain vanilla.

"This is so good!" Yusuf said.

"Honey Hill ice cream is the best!" exclaimed his Mom.

As they found a place to sit in the nearby park, people with their families gathered, on a busy Istanbul night.

Kids playing catch, some grown-ups were eating sunflower seeds while others were enjoying their ice creams.

"This is fun!" Yusuf said.

"We are glad you liked it," replied his mom and auntie, seeing that Yusuf was much better now.

After they got back home, Yusuf's mom gave him the special Yogurt Drink or Ayran as Turks called it. It is a popular drink in Turkey. And it was Yusuf's favorite since he was a little kid.

Ayran is also good for drinking before going to bed, it is soothing. Yusuf had it every day before bed. But this time Yusuf could not sleep.

Yusuf wanted to keep calm but he could not help. He had a great time with the family. But now, when he is alone, he remembered what happened during the day.

It took a while for Yusuf to calm down, only after he remembered the elephant story his mom told him. Elephants don't always go where you want. Enjoy the ride!

He felt sorry about himself since he forgot that when the elephant goes to a different place, you got to be patient and enjoy the ride and never make it a hell for yourself and for others.

He was so sorry for treating people bad over the dinner and especially his cousin Ahmet. He realized that knowing a principle and practicing them were different things.

He again made his nightly prayer, this time insisting more. Closing his eyes he repeated his prayers with a firm request.

"O, God, who has the keys of the secret gates, open me great gates," and went to bed.

Next day Yusuf woke up with full of energy. He had a good rest. When his mom called him to the breakfast, he wanted to make up his mistake from the previous night.

This time he was kind to everybody. Sort of making up for the previous. He had his usual breakfast, and he even ate the black olives he refused the day before.

By the way, did you know Turks eat black olives in the breakfast? Yes they do! But Yusuf was not used to it. Not this time. With a homemade olive oil and right amount of salt, it was not that bad.

He also had his usual boiled egg, Turkish feta cheese and most importantly hot Turkish tea. "Deliciousss!!!"

"Wooww" Yusuf thought when you change your mood, things around you change too. Everything around Yusuf, the food, the silly jokes, or daily politics they all seemed fine to him.

Happiness and joy of the people around made him happy. He enjoyed his time during the breakfast and tried his best not to let his mind slip into what he will do after the breakfast, persisting on his dream of finding Evliya.

After the breakfast he played with his cousin Ahmet. Yusuf was getting anxious about how he will escape to meet with Evliya. But he did not want to cut the play short since his cousin was also enjoying it.

Right around this time Uncle Mehmet came to pick Ahmet up to go home. This was surprising since Ahmet and Yusuf thought they had plenty of time to play.

Soon after Ahmet left, Yusuf made up an excuse to go upstairs to play with his other cousins, Kebi and Kayu. He had big plans, so he decided to have a fun night with them another time.

As soon as he left the apartment, he was right on his way to the Fatih Mosque again.

He walked three stories downstairs. He opened the front door of the building and closed it slowly since he knew it was a very noisy door.

Yusuf made a quick left turn and another one from the barbershop on the corner. He covered his head with the book of Evliya so that the barber would not see him. Otherwise he would want to talk to Yusuf and even maybe tell his parents where he went.

After he passed the barbershop, he ran towards the mosque. As it was not a bazaar day, on the way to the mosque, there were no vegetable stalls. He was lucky.

It was smart not to bring his scooter this time since this was much silent and efficient. He increased his speed and made another left turn right after he entered from the northwest gate of the mosque and ran to their original meeting point.

When he got to the area he found another bench, sat down, closed his eyes. He took a moment to stabilize his breath. Then he first said *Bismillah* and then "Travel, Travel and Travel" and Evliya was right in front of him.

"Thank God you are here," screamed Yusuf with a joy. "Where have you been?"

Evliya looked tired but happy. He said "well master, I was here last time too."

"How come I couldn't see you then?"

Evliya looked to his right over his shoulder and showed the area to Yusuf and said:

"Well, this place has changed a lot since the last time I was around. The last time I was here it was like a Pine Tree Forest full of trees, cats and puppies. Now I can't even recognize it myself."

"How do you mean?" replied Yusuf.

It was obvious Evliya was annoyed with his experience. The courtyard of the mosque was brand new clean marble tiles all over. It even had sprinkle pools too.

The area was great for kids to hop on their scooters or even swim in the recreational pools, although the security would never let them to swim.

Evliya was not happy about all the concrete around. He missed the old green space.

Evliya told the story of the Fatih Mosque and how he remembered it.

"When Sultan Fatih conquered Istanbul, he wanted to build a great mosque for the people, so he picked this location because it was one of the major hills in Istanbul. It had a breeze which kept the air fresh all the time."

Yusuf did not know the history of the mosque.

"During my time, when you sat on the courtyard trees would both give you shades and gathering grounds for people. The mosque was part of the nature and human life. There was a sense of connectedness between the people and the mosque," added Evliya.

"But now it is disconnected. I even myself got lost here," said Evliya returning to Yusuf original question.

"I went to the restroom where I saw this very strange thing. It was taking people up and down. I got stuck in it!"

"How do you mean?" said Yusuf.

"I do not know. It was this strange small room like thing going up and down. I have seen nothing like that before. When my mantle got stuck at its door, it was quite an adventure for me to save myself. By the time I was out you were already gone!"

"You mean the elevator?"

Yusuf was amused with this story. While he was crying the day before, Evliya got stuck in the elevator.

A traveler who traveled around the world thousands of miles, who overcame many harsh and intolerable circumstances but could not find his way out in an elevator? It was hilarious.

"So how did you find your way out?" asked Yusuf.

Evliya smiled hastily. "A seven-year-old Syrian kid was in that magical room with me. With a push of a button on the wall of... that thing... and that's how the door opened! It was like a magic. She saved my life."

"Seven-year-old kid saved you in the e-la-va-tor," Yusuf said bursting into a big laugh.

"Ok, whatever, elevator."

Upon seeing Evliya uncomfortable he realized that he had to change the subject and find a question, he struggled to find a question.

"Eee hhh, how did you know the kid was Syrian?"

"You know I can speak Turkish and Arabic and a couple of more languages. That's how I learned."

"So when you came out were you able to see his parents?"

"Her," corrected Evliya. "Her name was Yusra, and that's the sad part of the story," Evliya said.

"They were not there? What about her relatives?" said Yusuf.

Yusuf realized that Evliya did not want to continue to the story but Yusuf insisted.

"They... all... are... dead......" said Evliya.

"Dead?"

Evliya reluctantly continued on to tell the rest of the sad story.

Both sat silent for a while after Evliya finished. Then Evliya began again.

"In my entire life, traveling around the world, I have never seen anything close to what Yusra told me."

After Yusuf heard the story of what happened to Syrian people, he was shocked. He could not imagine how something like this would ever happen in another part of the world.

Syria and the US are on different continents, but that was the only thing he thought could be different between countries, not like a total devastation that happened in Syria.

He felt guilty as if it was his mistake. How could he have fun and do much stuff back home yet know nothing about the war that killed millions of civilians in Syria?

He learned that now there were more Syrians were outside of their countries as refugees, living in dire conditions. Yusra was one of those thousands of Syrian children living on the streets without food or shelter.

Evliya told him everything. Yusuf decided to learn more and read more about the issue when he returned to the US.

He could not talk no more. Yusuf asked for permission from Evliya. Evliya nodded.

Yusuf walked back home, passing by a toy store, ice cream parlor and the barbershop who even said hi to him. But Yusuf did not hear or see what was going on around.

When he got home, he wanted to just sleep and sleep. He knew he had to do something, but had no idea.

He thought about the Elephant's story. It made him calmer. Before he closed his eyes, Yusuf could say "O God, open great doors for men, women and children of Syria. Amen."

# IX. MEETING WITH THE REMARKABLE MEN

That night Yusuf had a dream. He was in his bed on a very dark night. He looked at the walls, it said 'Travel, Travel, Travel,' in old Turkish. As soon as he read the words, a white beam shot up in the room.

Yusuf stumbled back and collapsed out of fear. He was startled, but suddenly, the ceiling of the room ripped off slowly followed by a big loud sound.

Yusuf could see the full moon in the coal black sky. Then, Evliya descended from the sky together with a glowing white man with falcon wings only ten times bigger.

They came swooping down with a power landing which made a huge crack on the floor.

The man looked up. Yusuf saw him as a kind-faced man with a black beard, beautiful hazel eyes, and a long dress with a turban.

"Evliya has interesting friends," said Yusuf with a crack in his voice. "Who is this person?

"Hezarfen Ahmed Chelebi," said Evliya. "I wanted you to meet with him. He is a remarkable person. He achieved many great things in his lifetime. I wanted you to meet with him."

Yusuf was confused. Hezarfen had the same last name. "Are you brothers?"

"No, no relation," said Evliya. "But we are like brothers. I am the first one to write about his great accomplishments."

"What did he do?"

"Do you want to learn?" "Yeeees", said Yusuf not so surely. Then with a blink of an eye, Hezarfen picked Yusuf and Evliya up under his wings and they began to rise together.

They hovered over the apartment buildings. Everybody was asleep. Evliya described Yusuf the places they saw on the way. He was the expert traveler, right!

They first passed over the Fatih Mosque and made a downhill flight to the east where they saw the historic Orthodox Church. It was the headquarters of Eastern Christianity.

From there they turned to West uphill to the Suleymaniye (Solomon) Mosque built by the great Ottoman Sultan Suleiman the Magnificent. It was an architectural marvel.

When they got to the Suleymaniye Mosque Yusuf saw that it was both overlooking to the amazing Galata Bridge on the Golden Horn, and also to the Asian Side of the city through the Bosphorus.

They flew by the banks of the beautiful inland waterway called the Golden Horn towards the Bosphorus, the waterway that divided Europe and Asia.

There were thousands of houses connected with narrow streets with lights glimmering all over making the night like a festival.

The city with lights looked beautiful especially when the hustle and the bustle of the day disappeared.

Yusuf saw the "New Mosque" right in front of the Egyptian Bazaar, world's greatest spice bazaar. As they passed the New Mosque, they crossed over the Golden Horn to the other side, Pera.

They flew over the five hundred years old Karakoy Synagogue. It was now the museum commemorating how the Ottomans saved the Jews from the Spanish Inquisition in 1492.

Hezarfen with a swing of a wing moved upwards, using a little help from the blowing wind as well.

Going upwards Yusuf saw a huge stone tower in front of them. Evliya said this is the famous Galata Tower. This was a round stone tower with a fantastic look.

Yusuf was expecting that they will fly over it to see rest of the Pera. But Hezarfen seemed going right towards it.

"He is going to hit it and hit it badly" Yusuf thought.

He tried to get himself loose so that he could go somewhere else, but where?

He was flying hundreds of feet up in the air, all the brick buildings underneath. This was becoming really scary.

As they got closer and closer Yusuf realized this was not a dream anymore. It was a nightmare!

Realizing that Yusuf was worried, Evliya smiled. Yusuf closed his eyes. He hoped that he would wake up from this nightmare before hitting the tower.

Right after Yusuf closed his eyes with his hands, Hezarfen with a swift move of his wings and his legs took his head up and landed them all to the balcony of the Galata Tower.

When Yusuf opened his eyes, he was standing right on the narrow bars of the balcony. He was going in between falling back or jumping inside the balcony.

"Oh my God!"

Galata Tower

But thanks to the help from Hezarfen, his new friend, he was able to jump inside with a big relief, to which Evliya responded with a crack of laughter.

"Traveling is full of wonders," he said. "That's what I like about it."

It was a great flight across different cultures and history. In just minutes he flew over many historical treasures like Churches, Synagogues, the bridge and I don't know how many mosques.

Yusuf began to enjoy the view from the balcony of the tower. Then Evliya gave some more information about his friend Hezarfen Ahmed Chelebi.

"Four hundred years ago from this very location," Evliya said, "my dear friend Hezarfen flew with his wings to Uskudar," pointing to Asia on the other side of the Bosphorus.

Yusuf was shocked. "With wings?"

"Yes," replied Hezarfen proudly. "I made them all by myself! After years of hard work and dedication, I became the first person to fly in the entire human history!"

"The distance from the tower to the other side is over six kilometers," Evliya added.

After a quick math, "Wow, he flew six kilometers! It is almost four miles," said Yusuf.

Evliya did not know what mile meant. "You Americans like to use your own system but yeah in the rest of the world we all call it six kilometers. An you are right, it is a very long distance for an individual to fly on his own."

Yusuf was very happy to join his new friends. He was also glad to learn about Hezarfen. Yusuf decided to read and learn more about Hezarfen. It must have been a very difficult process for him to accomplish such a great project.

The view was marvelous. The Galata Tower was on top of a hill with a panoramic view of Istanbul. It was a breathtaking experience for Yusuf.

Evliya pointed to the big sky scrapers and the hustle and bustle going on in another part of the city.

Yusuf lost his concept of old and new. What an amazing city he thought.

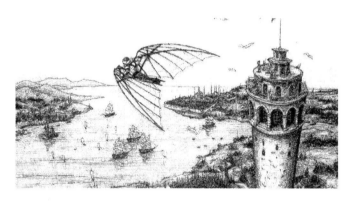

Did you know that Hezarfen was the first person to fly!

Later Hezarfen showed Yusuf another part of the city, a poor dilapidated section. Yusuf could see people sleeping on the concrete sidewalk without any pillows or blankets.

"Who are these people?" Yusuf asked.

"The refugees from Syria," said Hezarfen. He talked about the sad things that happened over the years. He explained how Syrians left their homeland to save their lives.

"They had to leave their homeland and go to other places, even to your country."

"Yes, I've heard about them on the news," said Yusuf.

"Although many of them are safe and secure here, it does not mean that they all have everything that they need. They still need jobs, food, clothing and money." Hezarfen whispered.

"Somebody has to help them," said Yusuf. "We can't just let them go through this."

"Nobody can do this alone. Nobody can do anything alone," said Evliya.

It was a nice city that promised a lot of things for the future. But the streets right behind those fancy buildings were home to many homeless people and refugees from Syria... kids on the street no food in their stomach. This made them all sad.

Evliya looked at Yusuf with a message to tell him.

"What do you think Yusuf?"

"I saved some money. I am going to share it with them."

"That's great but think big, Yusuf!" said Evliya. "Always think bigger. You have to have a bigger goal."

Yusuf had no clue how to have a bigger goal.

"Your mission," Evliya started in a stronger tone, "is to give and gain. Every major success that I have seen in the world in my travels both in the land of the Ottomans and outside of it, came with men and women working together for bigger goals."

Evliya sounded like a seventeenth century Ottoman bureaucrat talking with a royal tone ready to change the world.

"You can do this. You can invite other people to help."

Evliya did not want to sound flamboyant. But could not help.

"To change the world," he said "remember Yusuf, give and gain. In order to succeed you should be ready to give everything for your goal. Otherwise you become a mediocre person."

"What is mediocre?" said Yusuf.

It was a difficult term to translate in Evliya's old English accent. After a second, he said "average, just like anybody else. I don't want you to be average. You have to be a leader. World needs great people not mediocre ones!"

Evliya gave a break from his emotional talk. He wanted to do something.

Was this the reason Evliya emerged after three hundred years? Yusuf did not ask why he came back from history. He did not want the magic of it disappear and he also wanted to give Evliya time to settle from his emotional state.

It looked like Evliya was getting ready for a long sermon to give a message and before Yusuf knew it he began to tell his story. Like his books it was a long story.

"Yusuf," said Evliya "do you have a minute?"

"Sure."

"When I was growing up in Istanbul," Evliya said "I was living right behind this neighborhood. I used to come here visit places, go to mosques around here," directing his finger towards an old mosque.

"I saw the Holy Prophet Muhammad in my dream right there at that mosque," he said turning to the west side of the tower.

"You did?" exclaimed Yusuf.

"Yes," said Evliya. "I thought you already knew! It was at the Akhi Chelebi Mosque."

"O ooo. Another Chelebi," Yusuf said.

"I had many contacts in the royal family", showing the Topkapi Palace just to the south west of where they were standing.

"It was a very appealing life. People admired my situation. They wanted to be in my place. I could go to the Palace and meet with the Sultan whenever I wanted. I was even his Muezzin who called the prayers in the mosque for him. He loved me so much so that he could come and ask me advice on certain matters."

"I had a great life. But I had bigger dreams. I wanted to see different places and meet with people. I believed there is a world beyond Istanbul. That's how I was able to travel and write the longest travelogue in the world."

Hezarfen approached, "I think we have to go" he said.

Evliya concluded with a last message. "Don't be afraid to think bigger. History is written by those who think bigger not by mediocre ones!"

Evliya gave Yusuf a goodbye hug. He stayed at the balcony while Hezarfen took Yusuf back to his home.

Under the wings of Hezarfen, Yusuf looked ahead to the horizon thinking and dreaming about his life.

As he got closer to the home Hezarfen slowed down and made a sign with his head giving a signal as if he wanted him to jump down.

"Really?" said Yusuf.

"Sure, why not?"

After all the things he experienced, jumping did not sound scary. So he did it.

He fell towards the top of the apartment and passed through the roof to his room towards his bed. As soon as he hit his own bed Yusuf woke up with a dripping sweat.

He looked at the clock. It was three in the morning. Yusuf looked around the room, he saw a book on the floor. He quietly leaned down to see it. It was the 'Book of Travels.' He picked it up and hid it under the mattress. He was so excited.

# X.   FAMILY TIME

When he woke up Yusuf had many ideas. The stuff that he experienced in the night inspired him in a lot of ways. He got the idea that he should persist and try one more time.

He needed to find Evliya. He wanted to learn what to do. So while everyone was still sleeping, Yusuf put a blanket over his pillow on his bed to make it look like he was still in the bed.

He stealthy sneaked from the bedroom, and through the kitchen. But while he was still crouching, he accidentally hit a pot on the kitchen countertop, which hit other pots and made a crashing noise.

"Oh no!" He thought.

He quickly dived on the floor into one of the cabinets and shut the cabinet door.

Just when he did that, he heard his aunt.

"Who's there?! Oh. It was probably a bird hit the window and made the pot fall to the floor!"

After putting the pot on the countertop, she went back to sleep.

Yusuf quietly sneaked out again. Then he crept to the door and flung it open, in case, if you didn't know, pulling the door slowly makes a loud creaking noise, while quickly doesn't make a noise at all.

Then he quickly closed it and sat on the stairs. Taking Evliya Chelebi's book out he said "Travel, Travel, Travel!"

Then suddenly a white beam filled the stairs. "You called me, Master Yusuf?" Evliya in his beautiful turban with a mustache said.

"Yes, Evliya since we met last time I am thinking about going on my own and find some Syrian refugees and help them myself."

"Great idea Master." Evliya replied. "I will go out with my cousin and teach him also about this great idea about helping others. It would be great if you can join us," Yusuf briefly explained to Evliya.

"Alright master, it is then settled." He answered.

But suddenly, a voice was coming from the apartment where Yusuf's family lived.

"Who's there?" He heard.

"Quick! Evliya, disappear!" Yusuf commanded quickly.

Evliya then disappeared. Yusuf ran down the stairs, but he only made a few steps when he tripped and flipped over the rails!

"NO!" He screamed in his head! He quickly grabbed one of the rails as he was falling down from the stairs.

His reflexes had just helped him make it through. Then he heard his Aunt's voice as he was clinging on the rail.

"Strange things going on here, it was probably a cat. Everyone else is sleeping."

Then she closed the door and went back in telling Yusuf's uncle not to forget to close the building door next time so that cats would not enter the building.

Yusuf threw one arm over the rail and then the other. He landed back on the stairs and gasped for a breath. Then he ran up the stairs and tried to open the door. It was locked!

"Oh, come on!" He said to himself quietly. He used his brain and then suddenly found a paperclip on the floor.

"Yes!" He thought. He took the paper clip and opened it to its full length. Then, he stuck the pin through the keyhole and twisted.

He tried a couple of times but the door remained still locked! He was disappointed since this would be the way doors opened in the movies.

He remembered from the last time he was in town how his Aunt would leave the key under the mat so that if somebody left outside would open the door.

He simply took the mat up and here it is the key. He put it into the lock and it click opened. He felt great as he flung the door open.

He put the key under the mat. He quietly stepped inside and closed the door fast. Then he snuck back into his room and into bed to continue his sleep.

It was all between dreams and reality and sometimes he himself got confused to see what is a dream and what is the reality.

The next day, Yusuf's older cousins that lived the apartment upstairs came to visit them. After that, Yusuf's uncle that lived a floor below with Yusuf's other cousin.

It was almost like a family reunion. Everyday somebody came to say hi. They had fun all day. This was a great culture here.

People were so connected to each other. Many of them just showed up unannounced.

This created a big problem for the kids. They could not play in the living room because anybody could show up anytime. It was clean and crispy always.

It was a nice bargain. You cannot play in the living room but you have a lot of guests and you get to play with their kids.

At night, Yusuf and his Grandpa watched a TV series called "The 80s Show," like they used to do for the last couple of years. It was about the life in Turkey during the 80s.

As an engineer, his Grandpa explained Yusuf the differences between then and now. Learning the stuff happened in the past and comparing them with the current events gave Yusuf a perspective.

It was the same feeling he got from Evliya. Evliya taught him a different perspective about life.

It was a nice feeling for Yusuf since he already had this amazing experience with Evliya who literally traveled from three hundred years ago to teach him important stuff that mattered for the life of everybody.

Evliya was a great friend. He gave Yusuf the love for history and cultures which made Yusuf try new things and enjoy with different customs when he went places.

So, during his stay Yusuf watched local movies, tasted local food even he did not like the taste of some.

He wanted to try everything local so that he can teach other people who don't know about this stuff.

So, when Ahmet came with his dad, they thought about what they would do next.

"How about we go to the Big Slide?" asked Ahmet

"Good idea!" Yusuf answered. Yusuf went to his grandpa and asked him.

"Grandpa, can we go to the Big Slide together?"

"Of course," replied Grandpa.

Mom also joined them. They all went to the park. Ahmet and Yusuf went on the massive wide and long slide, then, Yusuf went, but suddenly, he slipped and lost his balance.

Before he hit two other people, he quickly turned on his side in a sliding motion. He barely missed hitting another person by inches.

He slid down and jumped on a bump and flew in the air a little. When he got down, another kid was coming towards him! He jumped a split second before the kid could hit him, almost causing him to flip over.

"What a ride!" He called to Ahmet. Ahmet smiled. When he got up, he slid down the slide almost hit another person, but hit three other people instead, crashing and the three kids were on the floor, in pain.

When they came back home, Ahmet had an idea. "Do you want to go upstairs and get the blocks and we build our own city with them?"

"Great idea, Ahmet!"

They walked up the stairs all the way to the top floor. They went to the small closet and got the foamy, colored blocks.

The living room had a huge carpet with a circle curling in to another circle. There were also peach colored sofas next to it. Behind them was a black dinner table.

"Do you prefer to play on the table or on the floor?" Yusuf asked.

"On the floor," Ahmet answered.

"Let's make our own city using some features of Turkey and using some of this city's features." Yusuf suggested.

"Ok let's do it" came the answer.

They first started building the city entrance, with arches and bridges. Then, they built a few towers with square blocks.

Then, Yusuf built a long, round tower. While his parents watching with wonder, he said this is my Galata Tower.

Everybody looked each other with a surprise. How could Yusuf know the Galata Tower?

# XI. HELPERS

The next day after he ate his breakfast Yusuf asked Grandpa if it would be ok to go in the city with Ahmet. Grandpa was not sure. They were so young for that.

Yusuf explained what he learned about the Syrian refugee problem in Turkey.

"How did you learn about it?" Grandpa asked.

Yusuf did not tell the entire story. He told him about all the news channels covering the issue. He was right, everybody was talking about it.

Grandpa asked where Yusuf wanted to go.

"Galata Tower."

"Why?"

"There are a lot of refugees there."

"Now I know how you built the Galata Tower last night," said Grandpa.

"Yep," said Yusuf. He told Grandpa about the importance of helping others.

They needed to do something and they could just start with collecting money and giving it to the refugees, especially the little ones.

It made sense to the Grandpa. He was so proud of Yusuf for his consideration. He invited all the relatives from the building and asked Yusuf to explain his project.

Yusuf talked about the situation in the Galata Tower area and explained how some refugees were living in dire conditions. He said he is collecting money to give poor and needy.

Everybody loved the idea and chipped in for this great cause. Yusuf counted all the money, it was 1610 liras. It was a lot money.

It was time for Yusuf to go to Galata Tower. Soon Yusuf and Ahmet walked out of the apartment, he took half of the money he collected and gave the other half to Ahmet.

Yusuf was thinking about taking the bus. But upon hearing this great idea, his other Aunt Narmin and her husband Husayin wanted to be part of this great project. They volunteered to give a ride to Yusuf and Ahmet.

Galata Tower was close to where Aunt Narmin lived so they also invited the entire family to join them for dinner afterwards.

It was a great idea. This way, Yusuf would get to see his lovely cousins, Jaylin and Omar. They all jumped into Uncle Husayin's van and headed towards their destination.

Yusuf named this project Mission Istanbul.

On the way Yusuf shared the things he learned from Evliya with Ahmet. He mentioned the poverty problem, and the refugees. To his surprise, Ahmet did not know much about it. But he was willing to learn and help.

Yusuf gave the directions to Uncle Husayin. In less than thirty minutes they all arrived at the place Evliya showed Yusuf in the dream.

Yusuf told everybody to follow him. He jumped out of the car since he remembered the area by heart. Everybody was surprised that Yusuf knew the area.

Yusuf passed a bakery and saw a Syrian poor looking refugee girl on the street. Yusuf and Ahmet stopped in her tracks and looked at the store.

Yusuf saw that the girl had no money as she asked for free bread from the shop owner.

The shop owner was rude. He said "I can't help all of you! I have already given ten free breads today. Now go away!"

Yusuf was heartbroken. He walked over the two people and offered to help.

"Mind your own business little child! This is only between this kid and me!" He demanded.

But Yusuf was going win this argument. "If she can't feed herself and her family, she'd die. You know their situation, right?" He said as a comeback.

The baker thought for a moment. "I know. But somebody has to pay for it."

"I'll volunteer for that." Ahmet replied. He took out three Turkish liras and gave it to the baker.

The little girl was watching them. Yusuf turned to her and introduced himself.

"My name is Yusuf, what's yours?" He hoped to learn about the refugees.

"My name is Yusra. Thanks for helping me," she answered with a broken Turkish.

Yusuf realized that she had the same name with the girl who helped Evliya at the elevator. It was like paying back time.

"No problem Yusra, I help people all the time."

"Where do you live?" Ahmet asked.

"I live down in the alley next to the High School," she answered.

"Could you help us finding other Syrian families around here?" Ahmet asked. She gladly volunteered. With the help of Yusra, Ahmet and Yusuf spent the rest of the day giving money and helping the poor and needy in the area.

They were exhausted. Finally they found a space and sat by the old Galatasaray High School. Yusra thanked Yusuf and Ahmet.

"Well, I guess you can make it from here. It was nice meeting you, Yusra," said Ahmet.

He checked his pocket and found the last hundred lira bill.

"Oh, and uh if you want you can take this."

He took out hundred Turkish liras and gave it to her.

Her eyes filled with happiness. "*Shukran Kathiran! Barakallah fikoma! Jazakallah!*" She turned and ran to where she lived.

Yusuf was happy to see how Ahmet helped Yusra.

When Yusuf and Ahmet reached aunt Narmin's home that night, they were tired but joyful.

All the family got together and listened to Yusuf and Ahmet's story.

They all celebrated the good deeds.

Grandpa called Ahmet and Yusuf. He gave them two gold coins each.

"Yay!"

"You deserved it."

# XII. THE MISSION THAT NEVER ENDS

After Yusuf had his dinner, he excused himself to his little cousin Jaylin's room to have some rest.

He locked the door and repeated "travel" three times. A white beam filled the room with light.

"Salaam, Evliya" Yusuf whispered.

"Salaam, Yusuf. Why are we whispering?" Evliya asked.

"Everyone's awake," Yusuf replied.

"Oh, ok."

Evliya was on a hurry.

"Congratulations for the all the things you have done today," Evliya said.

"Oh, thank you!" Yusuf responded back.

Before Yusuf could continue to talk about each and every great thing that they did that day, Evliya continued with a smile.

"*Mashallah*! But there are a lot of people who need your help," Evliya said "there is no time to talk about your past accomplishments, we need to start working on the future projects."

Yusuf was surprised. He thought Mission Istanbul was his first and last project.

"The past is already gone!" Evliya added. "Therefore, there is one more thing I need to show you."

"What do you mean?" Yusuf asked.

Evliya's answer was quick.

"Here, let me show you!"

Evliya grabbed Yusuf and said "*Imagination*!"

Everything started spinning.

Yusuf realized Evliya was taking him to his mind and his time.

"Where are we goi-?

To be continued….

## ABOUT THE AUTHOR

Yusuf Kerem Sahin, like the main character of the *Yusuf Around the World* series, was born in Miami, FL. He lives in Towne Square, a magical town just outside of Atlanta, GA.

*Yusuf Around the World: Mission Istanbul* is his debut book. Currently Yusuf is finishing his second book on World War II.

If you want to a receive a free chapter from Yusuf's second book, and learn how Yusuf writes his books, send an email to info@YusufAroundTheWorld.com or subscribe to his private readers group at YusufAroundTheWorld.Com.

66952721R00064

Made in the USA
Middletown, DE
16 March 2018